First published in the United States, Great Britain, Canada, Australia, and New Zealand
in 2009 by North-South Books Inc., an imprint of NordSüd Verlag AG, CH-8005 Zürich,
Switzerland. Distributed in the United States by North-South Books Inc., New York 10001.

Library of Congress Cataloging-in-Publication Data is available.
ISBN: 978-0-7358-2258-0 (trade edition).
10 9 8 7 6 5 4 3 2 1
Printed in Belgium

www.northsouth.com

FSC
Mixed Sources
Product group from well-managed
forests and other controlled sources
Cert no. BV-COC-070303
www.fsc.org
© 1996 Forest Stewardship Council

THE Smallest Snowflake

Bernadette Watts

NorthSouth
New York / London

Long ago, in a land where villages nestled between tall mountains, another winter was coming. High in the sky, geese were flying south. Higher still, snowflakes were gathering.

"Where will we go?" asked one snowflake excitedly. "Who can say?" said another. "Wherever the wind blows us," said a third.

"To someplace special," whispered the Smallest Snowflake very softly.

A little wind sprang up, whistling through the bare winter trees, bending the tall pines, running away with children's kites. The snowflakes began to drift and dance.

"It's time!" they whispered. At last they were on their way. Down they floated, merrily flying over the fields, into the forests, onto the red roofs. Soon the villages were covered in white.

"I am not staying here!" said one snowflake. "I'll ride the wind to the most beautiful mountain in the world. There I will sit, at its very top, so that everyone can look up and admire me."

"I am going to find a great forest," said another snowflake. "There I will sit on a branch and dazzle the bear and the squirrels and all the creatures of the forest."

"How boring," said another snowflake. He was larger than the others and felt very important. "I will travel many miles, until I reach a great city of jeweled domes and sparkling palaces. There I will sit on the tallest spire, where my beauty will outshine every jewel."

The Smallest Snowflake listened in awe to all these grand plans. She longed for a special place of her own. But where could that be?

The winter wind blew stronger. The Smallest Snowflake looked down and saw great ships on the ocean and tired little fishing boats asleep in the harbors. The snowflakes scattered this way and that. Some settled on cottage roofs, others clung to castle walls. But the Smallest Snowflake drifted on. No place seemed to be waiting just for her.

Some of the snowflakes said, "Come with us. We're going to a land where people live in ice houses and catch fish through holes cut in the icy sea. Our cousins are already there. They will give us a great welcome."

But the Smallest Snowflake knew that could never be her own special place.

The wintry wind carried her through the night, over wild and rocky places, across windswept moors, until dawn touched the sky. There, in the first light of day, she saw distant hills rising up with stone walls running down their sides. Geese called from a barnyard and people set about their morning chores.

Just below stood a little cottage with a gray slate roof and a red door.
Lights glowed through its windows and smoke curled up from its chimney.
The Smallest Snowflake settled down on a little window box filled with
earth and looked inside.

There was a fire glowing in the fireplace and a table set for one.
There were pictures on the wall and, on the table, a picture being painted.
The Smallest Snowflake had never seen such things before.

"This is a very special place," she whispered.

The Smallest Snowflake lay in the window box as the cold
weeks passed. Sometimes a woman came to the window and smiled
down at her as she painted.

One day the snowflake felt the tiniest movement beneath her.
Green shoots were beginning to push up though the earth in
her window box.

Day by day the sun grew warmer. Sunbeams played on the window box and the green shoots grew taller until buds appeared, as white as pearls. They were snowdrops, the first signs of spring.

Soon the apple trees and black thornbushes were covered with blossoms. Among their roots, primroses and violets flowered. Birds sang busily from every bush and tree. The window box was bathed in sunshine, and the snowdrop flowers all opened.

The Smallest Snowflake looked up at the tallest snowdrop. She had never seen anything so beautiful. Love filled her heart with such warmth that she melted away with joy. It was spring.